OKLAHOMA

ARKANSAS

North

Cimarron

North Fork

Washita

Little Rock ☆

Sal004

arillo

Palo Duro
Canyon

Prairie Dog Town

Fork

Red   River

Little   River

Red   River

Ouachita   River

River

MISS

Texas
Badlands

West   Fork

Double

Mtn

Dallas

Fort ☆
Worth

Brazos

Fork

Clear   Fork

Abilene

LOUISIANA

TEXAS

River

Llano River

Baton Rouge

Austin

Guadalupe River

Houston

New Orleans

San Antonio

Nueces

River

Rio

Grande

ICO

Palo Duro Canyon—from age to age the same.
Geologist's paradise. If Palo Duro could be fitted
on top of Grand Canyon all ages of the earth
would be stacked upon one place.

Palo Duro Canyon

UTE FROM
O AMARILLO

TEXAS
MADRONE

ATE LINE

Dear Brillo,
I've wondered where
the world

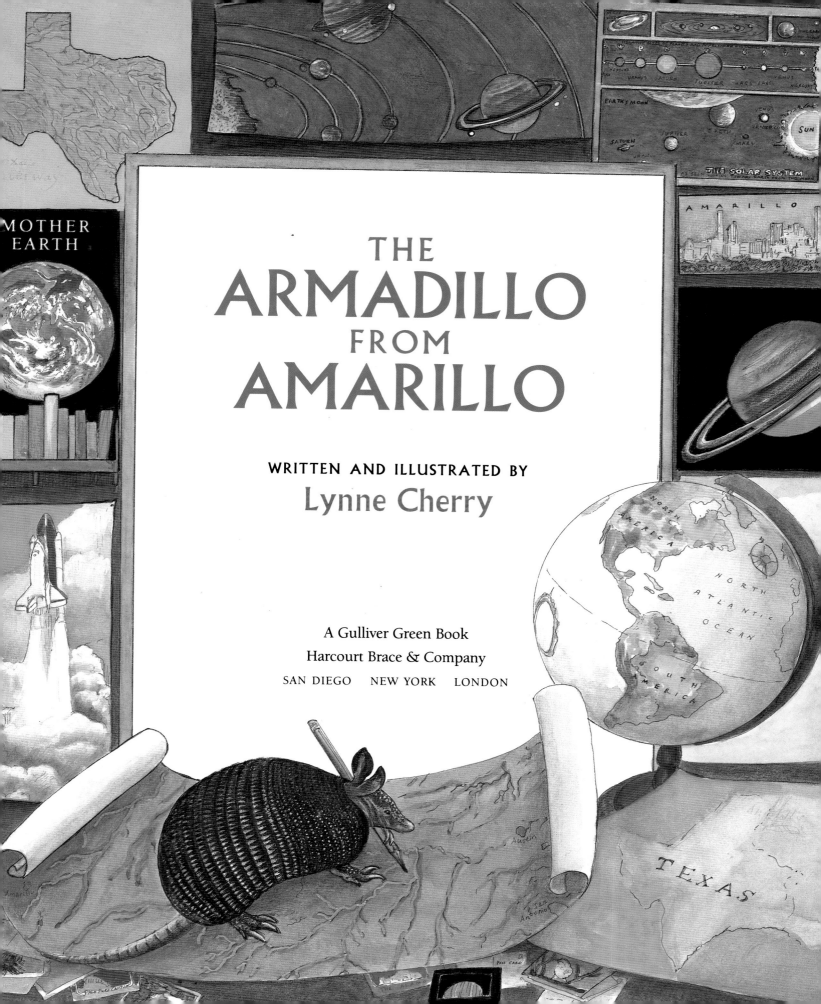

THE
ARMADILLO
FROM
AMARILLO

WRITTEN AND ILLUSTRATED BY
Lynne Cherry

A Gulliver Green Book
Harcourt Brace & Company
SAN DIEGO   NEW YORK   LONDON

Requests for permission to make copies of any part of the work should be mailed
to: Permissions Department, Harcourt Brace & Company, 6277 Sea Harbor Drive,
Orlando, Florida 32887-6777.

Gulliver Green Books is a registered trademark of Harcourt Brace & Company.
Stamp designs copyright © United States Postal Service. All rights reserved.

Library of Congress Cataloging-in-Publication Data
Cherry, Lynne.
The armadillo from Amarillo/by Lynne Cherry.
p.   cm.
"A Gulliver green book."
Summary: A wandering armadillo sees some of the cities, historic sites,
geographic features, and wildlife of Texas.
ISBN 0-15-200359-2
[1. Armadillos — Fiction. 2. Texas — Fiction. 3. Stories in rhyme.] I. Title.
PZ8.3.C427Ar   1994
[E] — dc20   93-11185

H G F E D C

Gulliver Green® Books focus on various aspects of ecology and the environment, and
a portion of the proceeds from the sale of these books will be donated to protect,
preserve, and restore native forests.

Printed in Singapore

The illustrations in this book were done in pentel watercolors
and oil pastel on Strathmore 400 watercolor paper.
The text type was set in ITC Berkeley Medium.
The display type was set in Albertus.
Composition by Harcourt Brace Photocomposition Center, San Diego, California
Postcards were hand-lettered by Judythe Sieck, San Diego, California.
Color separations were made by Bright Arts, Ltd., Singapore.
Printed and bound by Tien Wah Press, Singapore
This book was printed with soya-based inks on Leykam recycled paper, which
contains more than 20 percent postconsumer waste and has a total recycled
content of at least 50 percent.
Production supervision by Warren Wallerstein and Kent MacElwee
Designed by Michael Farmer

In memory of a kindred spirit,
Theodor Geisel (Dr. Seuss),
whose books have inspired
generations of children to
love planet earth

TEXAS ARMADILLO
This burrowing mammal is covered with a bony
shell. When attacked, the armadillo may roll up like a
ball and defend upon its own armor for protection.
Armadillos feed on fruits, roots, and insects.

SAN ANTONIO, TX
P.M
25 APR
1993

Dear Brillo,
I've lately had the
urge to go and visit
San Antonio, a city
I've not seen before
that my friends tell
me I'd adore.
    Sasparillo

BRILLO ARMADILLO
PHILADELPHIA ZOO
CHILDREN'S ZOO
3400 W. GIRARD AVE.
PHILADELPHIA
PA 19104

Distributed by Austin News Agency, Austin Texas

Photochrome
Irish brown

AN ARMADILLO from Texas wondered, "Where in the world am I?
What's out beyond these tangled woods? What's out beyond the sky?"
So Armadillo packed up his things and left his home behind.
He headed off on a northeast course to seek what he could find.

BLUEBONNETS
SAN ANTONIO
TEXAS

Dear Brillo,
Hi and warm regards
from your cousin
Sasparillo. I laid
my head and slept
today on a blue
bluebonnet pillow.
Love,
Sasparillo

BRILLO ARMADILLO
PHILADELPHIA ZOO
CHILDREN'S ZOO
3400 W. GIRARD AVE.
PHILADELPHIA
PA 19104

He traveled to the nearby city
of San Antonio,
and from the top of the highest tower,
he saw where he might go.

SAN ANTONIO, TEXAS
A bird's-eye view of San Antonio with the
Tower of the Americas in the foreground.

POST CARD

Dear Cousin Brillo,
I crossed the city and
climbed a tower, using
tooth and claw, and
looking down and all
around, this is what
I saw!
Love always,
Sasparillo

BRILLO ARMADILLO
PHILADELPHIA ZOO
CHILDREN'S ZOO
3400 W. GIRARD AVE.
PHILADELPHIA
PENNSYLVANIA
19104

I AM
HERE!

But Armadillo still wondered, "Where?
Where in the world am I?
What's out beyond the prairie grass?
What's out beyond the sky?"

THE ALAMO
San Antonio, Texas

Located in what is now the heart of downtown San Antonio, the Mission San Antonio de Valero, now commonly known as the Alamo, was originally located on the Rio Grande River and moved to San Antonio in 1718. Texas was part of Mexico until March 1836.

Antonio... the Jewel of Texas

Dear Brillo,
Here in San Antonio
there's an old fort
called the Alamo. It
reminded me that
long ago Texas was
part of Mexico.
Love, Sasparillo

ENDANGERED
SONGBIRDS

Black-capped
vireo

Golden-cheeked
warbler

GOLDEN-CHEEKED WARBLER and
BLACK-CAPPED VIREO.
AUSTIN, TEXAS

THE GOLDEN-CHEEKED WARBLER
IS THE ONLY BIRD SPECIES
WHOSE ENTIRE NESTING RANGE
IS RESTRICTED TO TEXAS.
THEY DEPEND ON THE SHAGGY
BARK OF MATURE ASHE JUNIPER OR
CEDAR FOR NESTING MATERIAL.

AUSTIN TX 7 C
PM
29 APRIL
1993

Hello Brillo!
Today I shared some cheerful
words with a wild turkey and
other birds. Some are endan-
gered~very rare~there aren't
many anywhere. That's why
it's so important that
Texas saves this habitat!
Most sincerely,
Sasparillo

BRILLO ARMADILLO
PHILADELPHIA ZOO
CHILDREN'S ZOO
3400 W. GIRARD AVE.
PHILADELPHIA
PA 19104

He followed the river past twisted oaks,
through ancient juniper trees
shared by warblers and vireos
and Carolina chickadees.

The landscape changed dramatically
through woodland, towns, and plains.
Armadillo explored canyons
and walked through heavy rains.

ENCHANTED ROCK
AUSTIN, TEXAS

He walked for weeks and came to Austin,
continued west and north
to Abilene and Lubbock,
he hiked and sallied forth.

ENCHANTED ROCK
A sacred place of the
Indians.

Dear Brillo,
I much prefer the
night to traveling
during the day. So
sometimes I look for
a cranny or nook to
sleep the sun away.
Love, Sasparillo

POST CARD

BRILLO ARMADILLO
PHILADELPHIA ZOO
CHILDREN'S ZOO
3400 W. GIRARD AVE.
PHILADELPHIA, PA 19104

Armadillo often along the way
climbed up to higher ground.
He scurried up the canyon walls
and stopped to look around.

Howdy from Texas!

Dear Brillo,
I'm near Amarillo.
This land is cool and
flat! It's definitely
an inadequate
Armadillo habitat!
I'll be the only
Armadillo who lives
near the city of
Amarillo!
♥ Sasparillo

POST CARD

AMARILLO TX
20 JUNE
1993

BRILLO ARMADILLO
PHILADELPHIA ZOO
CHILDREN'S ZOO
3400 W. GIRARD AVE.
PHILADELPHIA, PA
19104

How different were the plains above—
flowers went on for a mile!
Armadillo decided to settle down
and stay there for a while.

But Armadillo still wondered, "Where?
Where in the world *am* I?
Perhaps I'd have a better idea
if I could somehow fly."

One day he asked the golden eagle
as she came breezing by,
"What can I do for a bird's-eye view
from up in the big blue sky?"

"Hop on my back," said the eagle.
"I'll fly you wide and far.
And then you'll see, eventually,
where in the world we are."

Upward and upward the eagle flew.
Armadillo held on tight.
"With my tail-tip curled I'll explore the world
from morning until night!"

PALO DURO CANYON
Near Amarillo and Canyon, Texas
The Lighthouse: The Best Known Formation
in Palo Duro Canyon State Park

Dear Brillo,
Except for the canyons like
this one here, this land is
flat, flat, flat! And
an Armadillo near
Amarillo should wear
a scarf and hat!
Love,
Sasparillo

POST CARD

BRILLO ARMADILLO
PHILADELPHIA ZOO
CHILDREN'S ZOO
3400 W. GIRARD AVE.
PHILADELPHIA, PA
19104

Palo Duro
Canyon
Amarillo,
TEXAS

Armadillo looked down below and asked,
"Where in the world *are* we?"
"We're over a prairie, and in the distance,
that's Amarillo you see.

"We've flown over the prairie.
We've flown over a town.
Amarillo means yellow, my dear little fellow,
and the prairie's all yellow and brown!"

"I see Amarillo," said Armadillo.
"Could we see all Texas, though?
And if we fly *higher* up into the sky,
could we see New Mexico?

"Or if we fly *higher* up into the sky,
could we see the entire earth?"
"Well, certainly, surely, if you hold on securely,
we'll try!" cried the eagle with mirth.

"*Amarillo*'s a *city*?" asked Armadillo.
To this the eagle replied,
"Yes, Amarillo's a city in *Texas*,
the *state* where we reside.

"And Texas is in the *United States*,
our *country* wide and dear,
on the *North American continent*,
which is on the *earth*, a sphere.

"This sphere is called a *planet*,
of nine we are just one,
and as we converse, in the *universe*,
these planets turn round the sun."

Armadillo held tightly to Eagle's neck,
afraid of a long, long fall.
From over his shoulder, with the air getting colder,
this is what he saw.

They flew so high up into the sky
that Texas they saw below—
the part they call the Panhandle—
and the state of New Mexico.

"With my tail-tip curled I'll explore the world!"
Armadillo said to his friend.
Through the clouds they twirled, in the wind
they whirled, and up they were hurled again!

And when they looked up they could see into space.
They'd flown up into thin air.
"It's hard to breathe here! I'd like to leave here!
Eagle, homeward let's repair!"

"We're very high now," said Eagle,
"on the edge of air and space.
The atmosphere's ending, we should be descending,
but what a remarkable place!"

"There must be a way to fly higher up,
bringing some air aboard.
Perhaps we should travel to Cape Canaveral,"
Eagle said as she soared.

As they spoke of Cape Canaveral—
the rocket-launching place—
a shuttle took off with a roar of fire
and headed out toward space.

Eagle had a brilliant thought
and whistled a happy tune.
"Let's hitch a trip on this rocket ship
and fly up to the moon!"

With a burst of speed the eagle flew
in the path of the rocket ship.
It took her and Armadillo aboard
and continued on its trip.

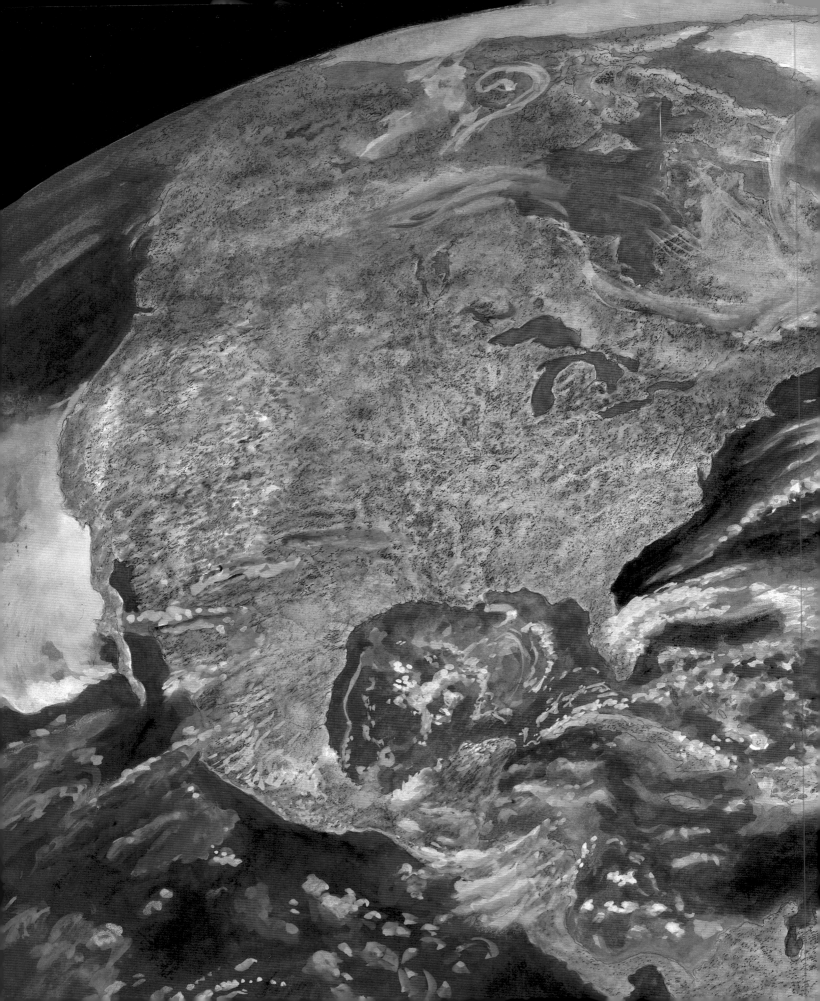

The higher they flew, the farther they saw—
Louisiana and Arkansas!
And there were some other countries below—
they could see Cuba and Mexico!

The spaceship then zoomed so high up
that Armadillo could not tell
where a country began or ended,
or where its borders fell.

The earth was now so far away—
so very, very far.
"I'm wondering," said Armadillo,
"where in the world we are."

"We're *out* of this world," said the eagle
to the armadillo, her friend.
"Ten miles from earth starts the universe
right at the atmosphere's end."

From space the earth was a big round ball,
with swirling clouds of white
against a deep-blue background,
like the blue-black sky at night.

Planets shone around them,
reflecting starlike light.
In that silent room floating in the dark,
they traveled through the night.

Before them was earth's silver moon—
a white and glowing sphere.
They hovered there, floating in thin air,
over craters, with no fear.

And as they watched in wonder,
the earth rose on the horizon.
They sat and gazed at their far-off home—
watched earth-set and earth-risin'.

Armadillo said, "I'm homesick.
Hey, Eagle, let's go back.
Let's go back down to our yellow town,
away from this blue and black."

The rocket began a downward arc,
then flew over land and sea.
The adventurous pair flew through the air
to their home by the yellow prairie.

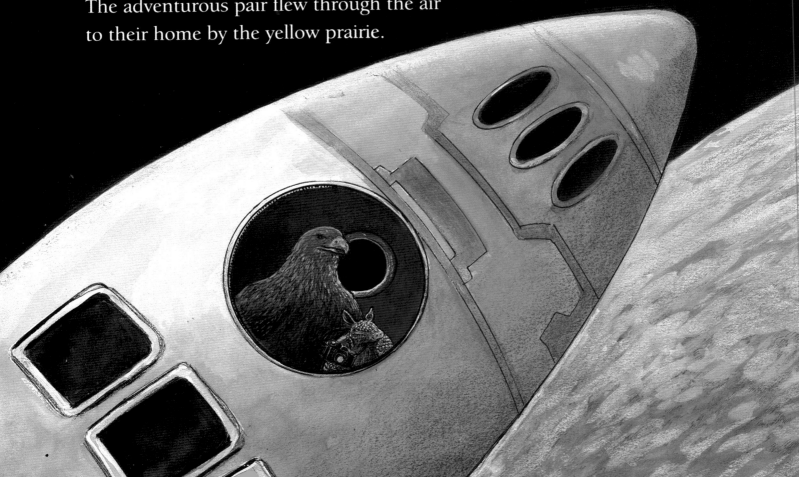

He'd wondered where in the world he was,
and now Armadillo knew.
He said, "I know where, in the scheme of things,
I am, Eagle, thanks to you!

"I now live near Amarillo,
a city that's rather small,
which is in the state of Texas,
one of fifty states in all,

"in the United States of America,
the country of my birth,
on the North American continent,
in the world, on planet earth.

"In all, there are nine planets,
and earth is only one,
and as we converse, in the universe,
eight planets besides this one
warmly, hotly, coldly, coolly
revolve around the sun."

Acknowledgments

I would like to thank the following people and organizations for their help:

Coy Batson, Harcourt Brace's sales representative in Texas, sent me research materials, many *Texas Highways* magazines, and postcards from all over the state bearing diverse stamps and postmarks. He drove me around to photograph the Texas countryside, explaining the Balcones Escarpment, the Blackland Prairie, and Texas vegetative zones. I cannot thank him enough for his assistance during my research.

Texas Parks and Wildlife Department naturalist Bob Spain drove me around the Austin area to photograph Enchanted Rock and the many bluebonnets, fire wheels, and other beautiful wildflowers that adorn Texas highways. He, too, provided me with excellent reference material, including copies of *Texas Parks and Wildlife* magazine. His help was essential to my understanding of Texas ecosystems.

San Antonio naturalist Susan Rust read the manuscript, gave me a crash course on Texas vegetative zones, provided me with maps of Texas watersheds, helped me conceptualize the book, and suggested areas that I should visit.

Astronaut Marsha Ivins of Houston read the manuscript and wrote me profound letters about her impressions of seeing earth from space and of the scars that our human civilization is leaving upon this fragile planet. I would like to thank both her and NASA for providing me with dozens of photographs of earth taken from space.

Ray Matthews, fisheries biologist/ecologist for the Texas Water Development Board in Austin, sent me many maps of and answered many questions about Texas watersheds and vegetative zones.

Donna Miller, art director of *Ranger Rick* magazine, provided me with reference photos.

Tom Van Sant of the Geosphere Project: Eyes on Earth, in Santa Monica, California, provided me with cloud-free computer-generated images of earth taken from space.

My mother, children's book illustrator Helen Cogancherry, shared her reference library and her artistic insights.

My father, Herbert Cherry, gave his technical assistance.

I would also like to thank Bev Gattis and Harry Everett of Amarillo and Tim and Merlin Cross of Austin for their Texas hospitality; Friedrich Wilderness Park in San Antonio for a tour of the oak-juniper forest, where I saw a real armadillo burrow; Claire Cuen of the Panhandle Plains Historical Museum in Canyon for her help with research; Lou Falconieri of Texas Natural Resources Information Systems in Austin for his help locating aerial photographs of Amarillo; Mike Strueber, aerial photographer, for providing me with aerial photographs of Amarillo; Sam Lovelady; Jim Werner of the Natural Resources Defense Council in Washington, D.C., and Dr. Geoffrey Parker of the Smithsonian Environmental Research Center in Edgewater, Maryland, for introductions to their friends in Amarillo and Austin; United Press International for its story in December 1984: "Test Finds U.S. Children Geographically Illiterate," which inspired me to write this book; Kim Whitman and Tanya Neff of the Philadelphia Children's Zoo for introducing me to Brillo the Armadillo; and Brillo, who posed for the armadillo in this book!

I would like to thank *Texas Highways* magazine, *Texas Parks and Wildlife* magazine, and the *Amarillo Globe News* for providing me with reference photographs and material.

Thank you to the following postcard companies, organizations, and photographers for allowing me to reproduce their images in this book: the United States Postal Service; Gilbert Palmer; the National Aeronautics and Space Administration; the Austin News Agency; Festive Enterprises; Jack Lewis/Texas Department of Transportation; the Baxter Lane Company; Wyco Colour Productions; Frank Burd; and City Sights.

Thank you to my friends at Harcourt Brace—especially my editor, Liz Van Doren; Rubin Pfeffer; Louise Howton; and Warren Wallerstein—for their loyal support and their willingness to print this book using environmentally sustainable publishing practices.

A special thanks to the Smithsonian Environmental Research Center for providing me with an artist-in-residency while creating this book, and especially to Mark Haddon, its director of environmental education.

And, as always, thank you to my husband, Eric Fersht, for his art direction and editorial assistance.

Armadillo (pronounced *ar-ma-DILL-o* in English and *ar-ma-DEE-yo* in Spanish) is a Spanish word meaning little armored one, and indeed, armadillos look as if they are enclosed in armor. This "armor" feels to the touch like stiff leather. It is made of narrow bands that slide over each other and enable the armadillo to curl up in a ball so that its vulnerable parts—head, belly, feet, and tail—are protected from the teeth and claws of animals that might want to eat it. Because armadillos' small teeth are in the back of their mouths, they cannot bite to protect themselves. Their best protection is in their burrow, where they live and can hide from danger.

There are several types of armadillos. The nine-banded armadillo is the only armadillo that lives in North America. Its relatives, the three-banded and six-banded armadillos, can be found in South and Central America.

Amarillo (pronounced *am-a-RILL-o* in English and *am-a-REE-yo* in Spanish) means yellow in Spanish. Many places and things in Texas have Spanish names because Texas was once part of Spanish-speaking Mexico, which was a possession of Spain. In 1845 Texas became part of the United States, but much of the Spanish culture and many Spanish names remain.

This story is about an armadillo named Sasparillo who wonders how big the entire world is and where his place on earth and in the universe might be. So he travels from San Antonio, in the south of Texas, to Amarillo, a city in the north Texas Panhandle. (If you look on a map at the shape of Texas, you can see why the top is called the Panhandle—it's elongated, like the handle of a pan.) Some of the things that Sasparillo experiences on his journey could not happen to a real armadillo. Armadillos could not actually live in Amarillo. They may travel that far north from time to time, but if the winter is colder than usual, they cannot survive there. Armadillos usually live in the warm climates found throughout the southern United States. They need a special habitat of scrubby underbrush, and there is not much of that in Amarillo. Also, in reality, Sasparillo would not be traveling during the day. Armadillos are nocturnal, which means they sleep during the day and come out at night to search for food. They dig for insects and roots with their long claws and lick them up with their long tongues.

An armadillo could not really climb onto the back of an eagle. Armadillos move by scuttling about and are not capable of wrapping themselves around something and clinging to it for a long period of time (like a monkey could). If you were to soar like the eagle and the armadillo, you would probably begin to feel dizzy from the lack of oxygen when you had flown about 10,000 feet up into the sky. Our fragile planet is surrounded by a thin blanket of air: earth's atmosphere ends only about ten miles up!

The eagle and the armadillo couldn't really hook up with the space shuttle above the clouds—the space shuttle would be traveling much too fast! Nor does the space shuttle travel all the way to the moon. But astronauts such as Marsha Ivins (who grew up a few houses down from where I lived as a child) do travel into space. Marsha has gone up in the space shuttle twice. From the space shuttle, astronauts can see only part of the earth. The only time astronauts could see the entire earth from space was during the Apollo flights to the moon, the first of which landed on July 20, 1969.

Although some of the things I've described in this story could not really happen, all the geographical information in the text is accurate. The story is meant to inspire you to be interested in discovering where in the world you are. Sasparillo learns that the world he knows in the tangled woods is just one of many. *You* can learn about where you are by reading books, looking at maps, and maybe someday setting off to see the world.